HarperCollins®, ⬛®, and HarperEntertainment
are trademarks of HarperCollins Publishers.
Madagascar: Escape 2 Africa: Lost in Africa
Madagascar: Escape 2 Africa ™ & © 2008 DreamWorks Animation L.L.C.
Printed in the United States of America. All rights reserved.
No part of this book may be used or reproduced in any manner
whatsoever without written permission except in the case of brief
quotations embodied in critical articles and reviews.
For information address HarperCollins Children's Books,
a division of HarperCollins Publishers,
1350 Avenue of the Americas, New York, NY 10019.
www.harpercollinschildrens.com
Library of Congress catalog card number: 2008930195
ISBN 978-0-06-144779-2
Book design by John Sazaklis
❖
First edition

MADAGASCAR
ESCAPE 2 AFRICA™

LOST IN AFRICA

Adapted by
Judy Katschke

HarperEntertainment
An Imprint of HarperCollinsPublishers

CHAPTER ONE

Even though it was colder than a polar bear's toes, the New York Zoo was packed with visitors.

"Tonight hundreds of New Yorkers have gathered to mourn the tragic disappearance of their beloved zoo animals," the news anchor reported.

The question on everybody's mind was, where are they now?

Where was Alex the lion with his winning roar and fancy footwork? What had happened to his friends—Gloria the hippo, Marty the zebra, and Melman the giraffe—after the ship carrying them back to Africa had disappeared?

But the answer didn't lie on the island of Manhattan. It lay on the faraway isle of Madagascar!

❀ ❀ ❀

"I like to move it, move it!" Alex sang as he shook his mane.

"He likes to move it, move it!" Gloria sang, too, as she shook *everything*!

Alex, Marty, Gloria, and Melman were having a major blast. Madagascar had turned out to be a lot more fun than they had first thought it would be, when their shipping crates washed up on the beach.

The jungle was ruled by a flashy lemur named King Julien. Music pulsated through

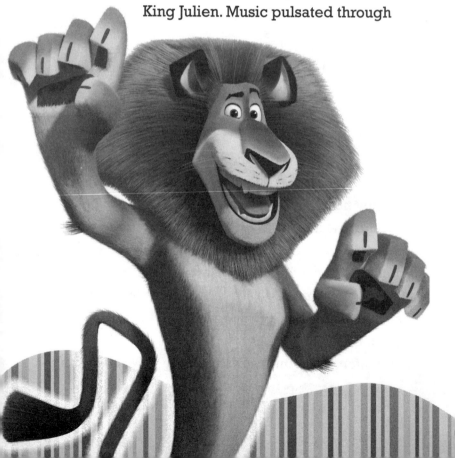

the trees as happy lemurs swung on vines, danced, and blew kisses in a glorious farewell party for their new friends.

It was time to hop aboard a rebuilt airplane and fly home. The New Yorkers took an elevator to a platform built into a treetop, where the plane was waiting for them.

"We're going to miss you little fuzz-buckets!" Alex said as they moved through a crowd of waving lemurs. "You guys have been a great crowd!"

A giant cake was pushed through the crowd by Maurice, King Julien's advisor. Written across the frosting were the words "Bon Voyage, Pansies!" But the cake wasn't filled with chocolate or strawberry cream. It was filled with King Julien wearing a coconut bikini top and gecko-decorated crown.

"Surprise, freaks!" Julien said, popping out of the cake. "Shake it, shake it, shake it!"

But it was King Julien's next surprise that would *really* shake things up.

"You will be very glad to hear that I am coming with you!" Julien announced.

Alex, Gloria, Marty, and Melman traded worried looks. Julien was one souvenir they did *not* want to take back to New York!

"No, thank you," Alex said quickly.

"Yes, thank you," Julien insisted. He then turned to the crowd and held up his gecko. "Until I return

with the spoils from the new country, Stevie will be in charge."

The lemurs grumbled as Stevie the gecko licked his own eyeball.

"I don't think they like that idea so much, Julien," Maurice said.

"Stevie says to let them eat cake!" Julien declared.

The crowd went wild. If there was one thing they loved more than dancing, it was eating!

Julien shoved the zoo animals onto the plane. After struggling to shove Gloria through the narrow hatch, it was NEW YORK OR BUST!

Alex, Gloria, Marty, and Melman made their way to their seats. Mason and Phil, two chimpanzees from the New York Zoo, were already buckled in, playing a game of chess.

The plane may have been shabby but the flight would be cool, thanks to its penguin pilots. From the cockpit, Skipper stared out the window at the second biggest slingshot he had ever seen!

"It's going to have to do!" Skipper said. He grabbed the intercom and announced, "This is your captain speaking. This is going to be a long flight!"

"New York City, here we come, baby!" Gloria cheered.

"We'd like you to sit back, relax," Skipper went on, "and pray that this hunk of junk flies!"

Alex blinked. *Hunk of . . . what?*

Co-pilot Kowalski fired up the engines. Outside the cockpit, Private demonstrated the emergency procedures.

"In the event of water emergency," Private told the passengers, "place the vest over your head and kiss your life good-bye!"

Melman gulped. He was beginning to feel sick— just like he did every single day!

Gloria wasn't worried, though. As the plane was launched by the giant slingshot, the hippo was already peacefully dreaming about the zoo.

But shortly after takeoff there was a problem in the cockpit.

"Skipper, look," Kowalski said. He pointed to a flashing red light on the control panel.

Skipper grabbed the flight manual. Then he reached over and smashed the light. "Problemo solved," he said.

"Sir, we may be out of fuel," Kowalski said. He pointed to the propellers outside the window. "We've lost Engine One. And Engine Two is no longer on fire."

Pilot and co-pilot buckled up. Soon a brand-new announcement was blaring across the PA system:

"This is your captain speaking. I've got good news and bad news. The good news is, we'll be landing immediately. The bad news is, we're *crash* landing!"

CHAPTER TWO

Everyone screamed as the plane began a spiraling nosedive. Marty was so freaked his zebra stripes practically zigzagged!

"This could be it, Marty," Alex called over the sputtering engines. "I just want you to know you're truly a one-in-a-million friend."

"Thanks, buddy," Marty gasped, his teeth chattering with fear. "You're the best ever!"

They were interrupted by Melman as he screamed at the top of his lungs: "I love you, Gloria!"

Gloria was still fast asleep. But Alex and Marty stared, wide awake, at Melman. They couldn't believe their ears.

"Um . . . like you love the beach, or a good book," Melman sputtered.

As the plane plunged, the animals went back to

screaming. But in the First Class section, King Julien screamed with delight.

"Raise your arms, Maurice!" Julien cheered as the plane dipped. "It's more fun when you raise your hands!"

Julien grabbed the handle of the exit door. The door snapped off its rusty hinges. Both animals latched onto a skeleton passenger, whose parachute popped open and pulled Julien and Maurice out of the plane!

"Long live meeeeee!" Julien shouted.

He and Maurice dropped toward the ground. So did the plane. But a second before it slammed into the dirt, it pulled up!

"Gear down, Rico," Skipper commanded. "You just want to kiss the ground. Just a little peck. A smooch."

The smooch turned into a screech. Skipper's hula doll wiggled wildly on the dashboard as the plane skidded across the ground. It ripped through trees, tearing off its wings and tail, before tumbling over a steep cliff!

"Commence emergency landing procedure!" Skipper shouted. "Flaps up! Deploy!"

The penguins popped open the plane's parachutes as it floated gently to the ground.

Oxygen masks dropped from the ceiling—or

what was left of it—and Gloria finally woke up. As
the passengers exited the plane, she looked around
with wide eyes.

"What happened to the plane?" Gloria asked.
"This is not the New York airport!"

Far from it! The plane had crashed smack-dab in
the middle of the African continent. There were no
high-rise office buildings, bridges, or highways—
only a vast savanna stretching out for miles and
miles!

"Good landing, boys," Skipper declared. "Who
says a penguin can't fly?"

The penguins high-fived each other with their

flippers. But Alex and his friends didn't get it.

"Hey, happy slappers, is there some reason to celebrate?" Alex demanded. "Look at the plane!"

"We'll fix it," Skipper said coolly.

"How?" Alex asked.

"Grit, spit, and a whole lotta duct tape," Skipper said. "We should be up and running in, say, six to nine months."

"Sixty-nine months?!" Alex cried.

But Skipper's feathers stayed unruffled. He turned to the chimps Phil and Mason and said, "Higher mammals—we can use your front cortexes and opposable thumbs."

Alex, Gloria, Marty, and Melman walked away from the plane gloomily.

"We're stuck here," Alex said.

Suddenly the lion saw something that reminded him of home. It was a safari tour truck packed with tourists—the kind of tourists that cheered for him in the city!

As the truck screeched to a stop behind Alex, the tour guide announced, "Behold the lion!"

Alex smiled as camera bulbs flashed in his face. If anyone would help them get back to New York it was people. After all, wasn't Alex the King of New York? But the truck lurched forward and started to drive away.

"Wait!" Alex shouted after the truck.

"Stop!" Marty called.

"Help us!" Gloria yelled.

More cameras flashed as Alex caught up to the truck. "If you stop I'll autograph those!" he shouted.

But instead of recognizing the King of New York, the tourists recoiled from the king of the jungle!

"Lion! Step on it! He's attacking!"

One gray-haired tourist named Nana did recognize Alex.

"I know you!" Nana snarled.

"You!" Alex cried.

It was the same lady who had once clobbered him in Grand Central Station. She had a big, heavy purse—and wasn't afraid to use it!

"It's the bad kitty!" Nana said as she whacked Alex over and over on the head.

"Owww!" Alex cried, grabbing Nana's purse.

Tourists snapped away as Nana and Alex traded kicks and punches. Marty, Gloria, and Melman could only watch and cringe.

After Nana kicked Alex below the belt, the fight was over. Then she hopped back into the truck.

As the truck zoomed away, Marty, Gloria, and Melman pulled an exhausted Alex to his feet.

"Are you out of your mind?" Gloria cried. "We need their help and you're harassing little old ladies!"

Alex held up Nana's stolen purse and smiled. "Who's out of my mind now?" he asked. Alex pulled out Nana's cell phone and dialed for help. But instead of getting the long-distance operator all he got was a recording that said, "The service user has roamed outside the coverage area."

Alex's heart sank. They were farther away from New York City than he thought. Where on earth were they?

"Guys!" Melman shouted. The lanky giraffe was

standing on the top of a nearby hill, pointing down to the other side.

Curious, the others scrambled up the hill. When they looked over to the other side, they gasped. Surrounding a shimmering water hole were herds of zebras, hippos, giraffes, and lions—just like them!

"I know this place," Alex said slowly.

"I think it's Africa, our ancestral crib," Marty said. "It's in our blood. I can feel it."

For Alex, it was more than just a feeling. He could sense in his bones that Africa felt like home. What he didn't remember was that as a baby he had been shipped in a crate to New York . . .

"MYSTERIOUS LION CUB FISHED FROM SEA!" newspaper headlines had screamed. The mewing baby Alex had been taken to the zoo where he grew up to be Alex the Dancing Lion.

That was a long time ago. Since then Baby Alex, Baby Marty, Baby Gloria, and Baby Melman had grown up to become BFFs. Now it was time for the best friends to meet their long-lost cousins! They approached the other animals around the water hole.

"Me Alex!" Alex explained as he pointed to himself. "Me and my friends fly in great metal bird," he continued, flapping his paws in the air. "Smash ground. Go boom!"

"Is he dancing about a plane crash?" a hippo whispered.

"You mean you came from *off* the reserve?" a giraffe named Stephen asked with surprise.

"Way off," Alex said. "From the New York Zoo."

A loud, ferocious roar made Alex jump. The roar turned into a wheezing cough as a middle-aged lion and lioness padded over.

Everyone fell silent before the hacking lion. It was their king and fearless leader, Zuba!

"What's going on here?" Zuba asked.

"They say they're from off the reserve," an elephant answered.

"That's impossible!" Zuba scoffed. "Only people come from off the reserve."

Alex couldn't stop eyeballing the lion. There was something familiar about this guy.

"What are you looking at?" Zuba demanded.

The lioness moved toward Alex. In a gentle voice she asked, "Alakay? Is that you?"

"No, it's Alex," Alex replied.

The lioness's gaze turned from Alex's face to the brown birthmark on his paw. "Zuba, look!" she exclaimed.

Zuba's face softened when he saw the mark. He stepped up to Alex and stared at him, too.

"All right," Alex said. "This is a little weird."

But then Zuba raised his own paw. There in the same spot was an identical brown mark!

"You've come home, Son!" Zuba said tearfully. Alex's jaw dropped as he looked from his paw to Zuba's. So that's why Zuba looked so familiar. He was his—

"—Dad?" Alex gasped. "Mom . . . and Dad?"

Zuba and Alex's mom nodded their heads.

Alex gushed happy tears. "I've got a mom and dad!" he cried, hugging his parents. He glanced back at his friends. They were crying, too!

"This calls for a celebration!" Zuba announced.

A warm, fuzzy feeling swept through Alex. He may have been lost—but he was finally home!

CHAPTER THREE

The four friends had a great time getting to know their wild cousins. Even Melman had a blast as he met his fellow giraffes.

"You don't have doctors here?" Melman asked with surprise. "What if you catch a cold?"

"We go over to the dying holes and we die," a giraffe named Harland said. Harland's neck pointed to a bunch of holes dug into the dirt.

"You guys really need a doctor!" Melman said.

"Would you be interested?" Harland asked.

"Me? A doctor?" Melman gasped.

Back home in New York he went to the doctor practically every other day. He was an expert on colds, achy joints, and stiff necks. All he needed was a clean white coat and a stethoscope.

A very, very long stethoscope!

✿ ✿ ✿

While Melman imagined his life as doctor, Julien imagined his new life as king—King of the Savanna. But as he and Maurice rode through the crowd on pink flamingos no one seemed to notice—or care!

"Hello everybody!" Julien called out. "Your new king is here!"

Lions in the distance still cheered for the return of Alex. But that's not the way Julien heard it . . .

"Maurice—I think they like me!" Julien cried.

The animals were having a wild time around the water hole, especially Marty as he hung out with his new zebra buds!

"Hey, you're a good-looking group," Marty told the zebras. Marty fit right in— every zebra was identical to him! "You like to run?"

"Oh, yeah!" one zebra replied. "Running is crack-a-lackin!"

Marty couldn't believe his ears. These guys not only

21

looked like him—they spoke like him, too!

The zebras thundered past a water hole where Gloria danced with other hippos.

Gloria stopped to watch a herd of males diving into the water with an enormous splash. They were big, gray, and handsome!

"Look at all the men!" said Gloria.

"Now how come you don't have a man in your life?" one hippo-girl asked. "Do you have worms?"

"Oh, I got rid of those," Gloria said. She planted her beefy hooves on her hips. "Listen girls. Manhattan is short of two things—parking and hippos!"

"Look out!" the hippo-girl said with a sly smile. "Because I think Moto Moto likes you!"

Gloria followed the hippos's gazes to the water hole. Her eyes landed on an enormous hippo rising slowly out of the water. Drops of water glistened brightly on his rippling gray folds.

Moto Moto smiled with twinkling square teeth as he made his way straight toward Gloria. "Goodness, girl, you huge!" he declared.

"So you're Moto Moto," Gloria said as they began to dance together.

"The name so nice you say it twice," Moto Moto said, chuckling.

Gloria tilted her head. "I kind of like it," she said coyly.

"I'll see you around, girl," Moto Moto said, smiling.

Gloria grinned as she watched the humongous hippo disappear into the crowd. It was then that she realized what the next best thing to being in mud was. It was being in *love*!

✿ ✿ ✿

The party rocked on. But for the first time Alex wasn't dancing. He was too busy filling his parents in on his life in New York.

"Hey, everybody!" Zuba shouted to the other lions. "I just found out that my son here is a king. The King of New York!"

Alex blushed under his fur. It was just an honorary title, really.

"Show me some of your moves, Son!" Zuba urged. "Come on, don't be bashful."

Alex raised his paws above his head and bared his sharp teeth, just like he had done it at the zoo!

"*Grr*," Alex said. "This one always knocks them dead."

Zuba threw back his mane and laughed. He had always dreamed that Alex would follow in his footsteps. And now his dream was coming true!

"You'll have my job in no time!" Zuba said. "Let's all welcome Alex back to the pride with open arms!"

The lions scooped up Alex and carried him on their shoulders. But not everybody was cheering. In the distance, another lion stood flexing his biceps. It was Makunga, Zuba's lifelong rival. Snoozing next to him was his enormous sidekick, Teetsi.

"That guy doesn't look so tough," Teetsi yawned. "You really think he could be leader of the pride?"

Makunga wanted only one lion to lead the pride—himself. So as he watched Alex an evil plan hatched inside his head!

"Not if he isn't *in* the pride," Makunga said. He made his way to the front of the crowd just as Alex was lowered to the ground.

"The other lions are griping about how Alakay never passed the Rite of Passage," Makunga told Zuba. "So technically speaking, he can't be a member of the pride."

"I had forgotten about the Rite of Passage," Zuba admitted.

"What's this 'Rite of Passage'?" Alex asked.

"It's a traditional coming-of-age ceremony where

young lions earn their manes by demonstrating their skills," Zuba explained.

"A performance?" Alex said excitedly. "Sort of a skill talent show?"

"Yeah," Zuba said.

Alex smiled. If he knew anything, he knew how to perform. This Rite of Passage would be a piece of cake!

"I want to do it!" Alex said. "Earn my mane, show my skills!"

"That's my boy!" Zuba said proudly. "We can hold a Rite of Passage first thing in the morning!" Alex was stoked. So was Makunga.

CHAPTER FOUR

While Alex prepared for the Rite of Passage, Skipper and the penguins prepared for attack. Dressed in leafy camouflage, the army of four watched and waited in the tall roadside grass.

"Operation Tourist Trap is a go," Skipper said. Rico peered through his cola-bottle telescope. A tourist truck rumbling down the road came into view. As the truck got closer Skipper ordered, "Stage one—go!"

Private darted out of the grass into the middle of the dirt road. As the truck screeched to a stop, Private added a dash of ketchup and a helping of egg yolk for the perfect roadkill effect!

After hearing a loud thud, the tour guide jumped out of the truck. "Oh, no!" he cried. "What have I done?"

"C'mon," Skipper murmured as he watched from the grass. "Take the bait."

Snapping their cameras, the tourists all climbed out of the truck and surrounded Private, talking all at once: "What happened?" "Is he dead?" "I think you killed it!"

Skipper grinned. Stage one had worked like a charm. Now it was time for—

"Stage two!" Skipper ordered. "Go, go, go!"

Skipper, Rico, and Kowalski raced to the empty truck. While the guide worked at saving Private with mouth-to-mouth resuscitation, Rico worked on starting the truck's engine.

VROOOOOM!

The truck was ready to drive. The guide had blown into Private's beak and filled up the penguin's belly with air. Like a balloon, Private floated out from under the guide and landed in the truck.

"Gas! Music!" Skipper ordered.

Rico popped a cassette into the player. While music filled the dusty air, the truck shot off.

"Stop! Stop!" the guide shouted. "Come back!" Skipper grinned back at the tourists chasing the truck. "Good work, boys," he said.

"What's all this rock and roll garbage?" a strange voice suddenly demanded.

Four penguin beaks dropped open as Nana rose from the backseat. The truck jerked to a stop, throwing the silver-haired woman onto the road.

Like a zombie, Nana rose again in front of the truck. Skipper stepped on the gas and the truck zoomed away from her.

"You hoodlums!" Nana shouted.

The guide and tourists caught up to Nana in the road.

"Okay, nobody panic!" the guide shouted. "The best thing we can do is stay together!" But Nana was already tottering toward the jungle in the distance.

"Where are you going?" a guy named Staten Island Joe called out.

"I'm too old!" Nana called back. "I'm not going to stay out in the open and get attacked by more animals."

The tourists exchanged worried looks. Then they followed Nana into the jungle. She was as good a leader as any. She had plenty of grit, spunk, and a pocket full of hard candies.

After they had traveled a while, a tourist from New Jersey screamed. She pointed to a clump of bushes in front of them that had started rustling.

Suddenly, a man stumbled out of the bushes. "Please help us! We're lost!"

More frightened tourists stumbled out. They had lost their truck, too!

"It was penguins!" one tourist cried.

"How are we going to survive out here?" another wailed.

Meanwhile, Nana was hunched over a rock, rubbing two knitting needles together. Soon she had a small campfire going.

"Calm down," she said. "In my day there were only three things you needed to survive: a square meal, a roof over your head, and a nice bath."

Staten Island Joe jumped up. "Is it just me, or is Nana on the money?! Let's build her a bath!"

The tourists went to work blocking the river with trees. They needed a fearless leader. And their fearless leader deserved a bath!

CHAPTER FIVE

As the sun rose over the crashed plane on the savanna, the penguins were already hard at work. They had stolen several trucks, which meant a ton of parts for the wrecked plane!

Rico busily torched one truck into two pieces while Private looked inside the hood. But Kowalski had disappointing news.

"Skipper, we have all the parts we need but we're slightly behind schedule," Kowalski reported.

Skipper glanced around for Mason and Phil. He didn't see them anywhere. This was not the time for monkey business!

"Private, what happened to our thumbs?" Skipper demanded over the PA system.

"Haven't seen them since yesterday, sir," Private replied as he fumbled with a screwdriver.

"Nobody goes AWOL on my watch!" Skipper boomed. "We'll track them down and bring them in for court-martial!"

"That won't be necessary," a voice said.

Skipper turned to see Phil and Mason. Behind the two chimps were more chimps—about a *hundred* more chimps!

"We've recruited a few extra thumbs for you, Skipper," Mason said smugly.

The chimps went bananas working on the plane. Skipper smiled as he watched the power of primates at work!

✿ ✿ ✿

It was all work and no play for the penguins and chimps. But later that morning Alex couldn't wait to play for the adoring crowd.

"So, little cub scouts," Alex said backstage to the other lions going through the Rite of Passage. They were all young cubs. "Just remember—a great performance comes from the heart, okay?

"Sure, Mister," the cubs snickered.

Makunga strolled backstage. He put his arm around Alex and pulled him away from the little cubs.

"In my opinion," Makunga said in a low voice, "the key to this whole thing is choosing the right competitor."

"You mean this is like a dance battle?" Alex asked. His eyes lit up. "Who do you think would be a good match for me?"

Makunga looked over both shoulders. Then he leaned closer to Alex and whispered, "If it was me out there . . . I'd choose Teetsi."

"Teetsi!" Alex repeated. "Thanks, Makunga!"

"Anything for Zuba's boy," Makunga said slyly. Suddenly—*Booong!* The sound of the gong was music to Alex's ears. It was show time!

Lions banged on drums as Alex and the cubs jogged into the ring. Alex waved to the cheering crowd. It was just like the zoo—without the peanut stands and gift shop!

"Let us begin the Rite of Passage ceremony!" Zuba boomed from his podium.

"C'mon, baby!" Mom called. "Make Mama proud!"

"On it, Mom!" Alex called back.

He and the cubs took their places in front of Zuba.

"Who will be first?" Zuba asked. "How about you?" Zuba said to Alex with a wink. "Choose your opponent."

Alex scratched his chin as he pretended to think. He didn't want his dad to know he had a hot tip from Makunga!

"Hmm . . . I guess I'll pick . . . Teetsi!" Alex said.

Gasps filled the arena.

"Why did he pick Teetsi?" Mom asked.

"That's my boy!" Zuba said, beaming with pride. "He's got gumption!"

Nearby, Teetsi was sleeping soundly. Another lion picked up a boulder and smashed it over his head.

"*Grrr!*" Teetsi growled as he rose to his feet. He flexed his enormous muscles as he lumbered into the ring. Looming over Alex, Teetsi let out an earth-shaking roar.

"Let's dance!" Teetsi snarled.

"Okay," Alex said, and he began tap dancing. Teetsi shook his mane and growled, "Not *dance* dance. Fight!"

Alex stopped tapping. *Hmmmm . . .* the only dance fight he knew was from a classic Broadway musical.

Snapping his fingers and humming a song, Alex broke into a series of fan kicks and pivots. Teetsi snickered under his breath. This was going to be easy!

For the big finish, Alex pirouetted into his final pose. But when he looked toward Teetsi his blood ran cold. His opponent was charging at him like an express subway train. He tried to get out of the way but—

Slam!

Teetsi plastered Alex against a boulder. The rock cracked in two over Alex's aching head.

"Oh, no," Zuba said.

"Alakay." Mom groaned.

The crowd watched in silence as Alex slid to the ground.

"Alakay has failed the test!" Makunga declared. "Who would have ever imagined that Zuba would have to cast out his own son?"

"Zuba, no!" Mom pleaded.

"But sadly, the Alpha Lion must cast out all failures," Makunga sighed.

Zuba looked at Alex. His son was finally home. How could he ever send him away?

"Then I am no longer your Alpha Lion!" Zuba declared. He held up his mighty scepter, then threw it to the ground.

"Dad, no," Alex said. "You can't do that."

Makunga picked up the scepter and turned to the

crowd. "Who could possibly take Zuba's place?" he called out. "Anyone?"

One lion began to volunteer, but Makunga swung the scepter, knocking him out cold.

"I guess not," Makunga said.

There were no other applicants.

"I suppose I could carry this tremendous burden," Makunga announced. "Teetsi—get the hat!"

Teetsi stepped forward holding a hat covered in fruit. It was the Hat of Shame! He slammed it on Alex's head.

Alex gazed up at the dangling pieces of fruit. He didn't need a goofy hat to feel like a fool.

"I order Alakay to leave the water hole and wear this Hat of Shame," Makunga boomed. "He shall be banished from the pride for a thousand years!"

And so by the order of the new king, Alex was banished to the bleak and deserted scrubland, and his parents went with him.

Alex looked at his parents. "I was the one cast out," he said, "Why are you moving out here?"

"Because we're a family and we've got to stick together!" answered his mom. But Zuba was angry.

"You should have told us that you weren't a real king!" shouted Zuba.

"Well, you never told me I'd have to fight

anybody!" said Alex. "None of this would have happened if—"

"—If you were a real lion," finished Zuba.

A real lion? The words hit Alex like a ton of New York pretzels. He hadn't made his parents proud at all. He had done nothing but disappoint them!

The anger was gone from Zuba. "It was my fault," Zuba sighed. "You were always different. If I had raised you, maybe things would have turned out better."

For Alex, it was the worst day of his life. But for Marty, back at the water hole, his day was off the chiz-ain! That's because he was wowing his new zebra buds with his famous water show—spitting cascades of water over the crowd.

"Ta-daaaaa!" Marty sang out. "Bet you haven't seen that before!"

"Let's all give it a try!" one zebra said.

Marty chuckled. A class act like his took years of practice!

"You don't just learn something like this overnight," Marty began explaining.

But the zebras were already filling up.

Marty watched wide-eyed as 500 zebras marched in formation. They started spitting cascades of water into the air like synchronized fountains. For the big finish they turned to Marty and spit the water all over him!

"Ta-daaaaa!" the zebras sang out.

Marty couldn't believe it. "You guys got it right out of the box!" he said.

"It's in our blood!" one zebra said.

"I always thought I was a little unique," Marty admitted.

"We are unique!" the zebras chimed. "Exactly the same!"

"Exactly the same," Marty repeated slowly. He and the other zebras looked alike and talked alike. But did they have to spit water alike, too?

CHAPTER SIX

If things weren't going great for Alex and Marty, at least Melman was at the top of his game!

The other giraffes had made him their Witch Doctor. Now he could use his medical smarts to heal his fellow giraffes! Plus, it kept him from thinking about his feelings for Gloria.

The other giraffes craned their necks to watch the respected Dr. Mankoweicz perform his latest operation—fitting a splint on a young giraffe's leg.

"You're in my light, Stephen," Melman complained.

Stephen leaned even closer toward Melman and said, "You've got a brown spot there on your shoulder."

"As you can see, I'm covered in brown spots," Melman said. He smiled down at his patient. "Okay, that bone will be as good as new in a few weeks."

As he turned, he noticed Stephen still staring at his shoulder!

"Uh," Stephen said. "This spot looks like Witch Doctor's Disease."

"Witch Doctor's Disease?" Melman laughed. "That's the most ridiculous disease I've ever heard of, Stephen."

Melman got to work on his next patient—an elephant with a tangled trunk.

"Someone's been knotty!" Melman joked.

But Stephen wasn't laughing. He was still worrying over Melman's spot.

"Our last Witch Doctor, Joe, had a spot just like that," Stephen explained. "Monday: Joe. Wednesday: no Joe."

Melman gulped as it suddenly clicked. His days were numbered!

"You'll find a cure," Stephen said cheerily. "You've got at least forty-eight hours."

Forty-eight hours? Melman did the math. His numbered days equaled two!

"Sandy," Melman sadly told his receptionist, "cancel my appointments."

Melman was still in shock as he untangled the elephant's trunk. Just when life was getting better it was about to end. It just wasn't fair!

✿ ✿ ✿

The lanky giraffe trudged to the plane-crash site, where Alex and Marty were hanging out. His friends looked just as bummed out as he felt.

"You know what? I've got to find a hole where I can die," Melman sighed.

Not understanding, Alex said, "You and me both, buddy. My dad thinks I'm a total loser. I've got to find a way to fix this."

"This is definitely not crack-a-lackin," Marty said.

The three unhappy friends were suddenly joined by a very happy Gloria.

"You're not going to believe it," Gloria said, "but I've got a date with Moto Moto!"

Alex and Marty were surprised. But Melman was positively dumbstruck.

"Who's Moto Moto?" Melman asked.

"Oh, he's so big and handsome . . . and big!" Gloria said. "Do you know what 'Moto Moto' means?"

"It means 'hot hot'!" Marty said.

Gloria and the others stared at Marty. Since when did he speak African?

"You can flirt with Mr. Hot Pants after I'm gone," Melman said angrily.

"What's the deal, Melman?" Gloria snapped. "Why am I the parade and you're the rain?"

"Why do you have to drive your parade under my rain?" Melman demanded.

"Maybe I'll just parade myself in another part of town!" Gloria snapped.

Alex couldn't take it anymore. "Melman!" he said. "Why don't you just tell her?"

Melman froze. No way could he tell Gloria he loved her. Not with Mr. Hot Hot in the picture!

"I don't know what you're talking about!" Melman said.

Gloria stormed off one way, Melman the other.

"Hey!" Marty shouted after them. "I thought you guys were friends!"

"Marty is right!" Alex called.

Just then Alex and Marty were joined by another zebra—the *real* Marty!

"What the heck is going on?" Marty asked.

Alex looked from one identical zebra to the other. "I thought . . . he was—"

"You thought that guy was me?!" Marty cut in.

"You guys do kind of look a little . . . you look a lot alike!" Alex admitted.

"So you're saying there's nothing unique about me," Marty said. "I'm just like any other zebra."

"I can't tell you apart," Alex admitted. "Maybe you should wear a bell or something."

Marty turned on all fours and stomped away.

Alex's heart sank as he stood all alone. How could he go home to New York without his best friends?

Melman made himself a new home in a giraffe dying hole. As

he lay in the dirt his sad eyes hardly noticed Julien and Maurice riding by on a pair of ostriches.

"Oh!" Julien said, staring at Melman. "Who would leave a perfectly good head lying around?"

"What a waste," Maurice sighed.

"Tell me about it," Melman sighed. "I probably have another two days left. Tops."

That didn't jive with King Julien!

"If I, King Julien, only had two days left," Julien said. "I would do all the things I've ever dreamed of doing."

Melman gave it a thought. "There is one thing," he said softly.

"What is it?" Julien asked. "Tell me!"

"I never really had the guts to tell Gloria how I feel about her," Melman confessed.

Julien's huge eyes lit up. He considered himself an expert on love.

"Now listen to me," Julien told Melman. "You've got to rise up!"

Melman stood up on spindly legs.

"You're going to go right up to this woman,"

Julien went on. "You're going to go right up to her face. And then you're going to say, 'Baby, I dig you!'"

"Yeah!" Melman cried, feeling the power. "I'm going to do it! I'm going to do it!"

✿ ✿ ✿

When Melman finally ran to find Gloria, she was already sitting under a full moon with Moto Moto. The moonlight cast a glow on her date's hefty gray neck. Sure, he was fine. But what did Moto Moto think of her?

"So what is it about me that you find attractive?" Gloria asked.

"You are the most plumpin' girl I've ever met!" Moto Moto complimented.

"Other than that," Gloria urged.

"My gosh, girl, you huge!" Moto Moto said.

Gloria heaved a big sigh. She knew she was a brick house. But wasn't there anything else about her that Moto Moto liked?

Moto Moto was about to plant a kiss on Gloria's lips when Melman burst through the bushes.

"Gloria!" Melman gasped.

"Melman," Gloria said. "I want you to meet Moto Moto."

"We're kind of busy here, man," Moto Moto said.

Sadly, Melman turned to leave. She was in love with someone else. And what did he have to offer? He had only two measly days left to live!

Melman stopped in his tracks. Then again, with only two days to live—what did he have to lose? Melman ran back to Moto Moto and looked him straight in the eye.

"You better treat this lady like a queen!" Melman said. "Because you, my friend, you've found the perfect woman. If I was ever so lucky to find the perfect woman, I'd give her flowers every day. And breakfast in bed. Six loaves of wheat toast with butter on both sides!"

Gloria stared at Melman. She had never heard her giraffe friend speak this way before.

"That's what I would do if I were you," Melman told Moto Moto. "But I'm not. So you do it."

A bunch of hippos rose out of the water to watch Melman walk away. "That was beautiful!" one hippo said with a swoon.

"Where were we?" Moto Moto asked Gloria.

"I'm huge," Gloria said slowly. But as she looked at Moto Moto, she had a feeling that she had made a *huge* mistake!

47

As the sun rose over the savanna, Alex walked alone, crying to himself. His best friend hated him. Even his own father didn't think he was a real lion!

Suddenly, Alex heard a piercing scream. He turned toward the water hole. But this time it wasn't filled with water. It was filled with mud as a fish flopped around gasping for oxygen.

"Oh, no!" Alex said.

More animals crowded around the dry water hole. They didn't know why the water was gone, they just knew they were doomed!

Makunga pushed his way through the crowd.

"What's going on here?" he demanded.

A dik-dik pointed to a tiny puddle at Makunga's feet. "The water hole has dried up," he said. "That's all that's left."

All eyes were on Makunga. He was their leader now. What would he do?

"We must work together to find a quick and practical solution," Makunga said. "Any suggestions?"

"We can fight for it!" Teetsi sneered.

"That's not fair!" an angry dik-dik complained. "You two would win!"

Things were getting hairy between Makunga and his animal kingdom. Alex snuck up behind them to listen in.

"Sorry, folks, but life isn't fair," Makunga said as he circled the water that was left, forcing everyone else back.

Stephen the giraffe piped up, "Zuba would know what to do!" The other animals nodded.

Makunga sneered. "Zuba stepped down. I'm in charge. Your best hope is to travel upriver and find out what happened to the water."

"Off the reserve?" an elephant cried. Any animal wandering off the reserve would get his head blown off by hunters. It was crazy!

Alex looked at the dry riverbed and thought for a moment. Then he straightened his shoulders and started walking upriver.

Bravely, Alex made his way to the border of the savanna. He was determined to save the water hole and his family. But first there was something he had to do.

"Marty?" Alex called out to the zebra herd. "I know

you're in there. I wanted to say good-bye and . . . you've been a great friend!"

Alex stared at the hundreds of zebras standing before him. They were all listening, but which one was his friend? It's true they were all identical, but Marty always stood out in a crowd!

"You!" Alex called. "Twelfth row, two hundred and third from the left. That's you, Marty! I know it's you!"

Alex waited a beat.

Then Marty stepped out of the herd!

"You know what makes you special?" Alex told his friend. "They're white with black stripes. You're black with white stripes!"

After a few more compliments, Marty smiled and said, "Okay, I'm in."

"No, Marty!" Alex gasped. "You can't come with me."

Marty never took no for an answer. "I don't believe you have a choice!" he said with a grin.

The two best friends walked off the reserve, side by side, into the dark, creepy jungle.

CHAPTER EIGHT

Back at the water hole, the animals dug desperately for any drops they could find.

"Any water?" Gloria called.

"No, just more diamonds and gold," Moto Moto sighed as he tossed an armful of gems on the ground.

All of a sudden Julien led a procession of ostriches and elephants to the water hole.

"Attention, everybody!" Julien called out. "There is only one way to get your precious water. I, your beloved King Julien, must simply make a small sacrifice to my good friends, the water gods, in the volcano!"

The animals listened as Julien explained. The sacrifice would go in the volcano. Then the friendly gods would eat the sacrifice and give them water in return!

"We'll do it!" the animals said together.

Julien asked for a volunteer.

"I'll do it," Melman sighed. "I'm dying anyway."

"Melman?" Gloria gasped. She watched in horror as the animals lifted the dejected giraffe on their shoulders and carried him to the rim of the volcano.

Gloria chased after the crowd. "Melman, what's wrong with you?" she cried.

"Gloria, I just want you to know," Melman said. "Back at the zoo it was never the doctors that kept me going. It was you!"

The crowd pushed Gloria aside as they carried Melman away.

"Melman, wait!!" Gloria shouted.

It was too late. Melman was already standing on the rocky edge of the volcano.

"Jump! Jump! Jump!" the animals chanted.

"Don't rush me!" Melman called back. He stood on the edge and prepared his high dive.

"Please, Melman, stop!" Gloria shouted. "You can't do this!"

"Why not?" Melman called back. Suddenly the rock beneath Melman's hooves began to crumble. Before he could scramble back the rock gave way, and he plummeted into the center of the volcano!

In a flash, Gloria reached out and grabbed Melman's neck. As he hung over the volcano she

said, "Melman, I've got to know.
Did you really mean all those
things you said about me?"

"Of course I did," Melman
said.

Gloria smiled as she pulled
Melman out of the volcano.
She went halfway around the
world to find love, and all this
time it was right next door!

"Whoa, what happened?" Julien
cried as he watched Melman and
Gloria hug.

"I believe the fat lady
has sung!" Maurice said.

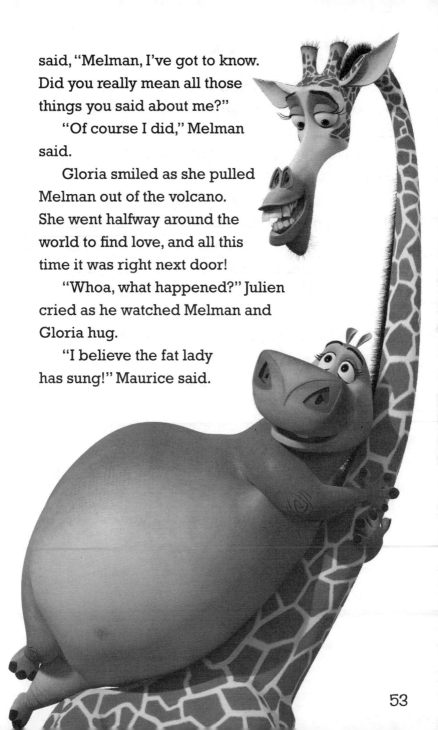

✿ ✿ ✿

Makunga and Teetsi just sat back by the water hole and watched all the commotion. There seemed to be zebras running around everywhere.

Some of them were on their way to Alex's parents.

Zuba was sitting on a log, moping. Alex's mom told him to go find their son.

"Go apologize to that boy!" she said. "You don't want to lose him a second time, Zuba." The old lion saw that she had a point, but he didn't know where to look.

"I don't know where he went." He shrugged.

"We do!" chimed in a bunch of zebras. A whole crowd of them had arrived and started talking at once.

"Your son took Marty upriver! Off the reserve!" yelled a zebra in the back.

Zuba gasped! That was dangerous! Zuba had to save his son from the hunters. His paws kicked up dust as he bounded straight for the jungle.

CHAPTER NINE

Alex's and Marty's eyes darted from side to side as they walked up the dry riverbed. They were surrounded by jungle.

Alex suddenly stopped in his tracks. He looked up and said, "Marty, this is it, the clog in the river!"

Both friends stared up at the towering dam of trees made by Nana and the other tourists.

"We're going to need more manpower," Alex said.

"Let's get your dad," Marty suggested.

"I was thinking of the penguins," Alex said.

Blam! A bullet blew off Alex's fruit hat!

Alex whirled around and saw a band of hungry tourists run out of the jungle. With a rebel yell the humans charged, shaking spears.

"Savages!" Marty cried.

"Evasive maneuvers!" Alex shouted.

Alex and Marty zigzagged, trying to dodge the tourists who were chasing them. Booby traps went off around them until—*Snap!* A snare yanked shut and scooped Alex off the ground by the leg.

"Alex!" Marty cried.

"Run, Marty," Alex yelled. "Go get help!"

Marty ran for his life back into the jungle.

Alex thought things couldn't get worse—until he found himself in the tourist camp, tied to a spit over a fire pit!

Sparks crackled as Nana lit the fire. Alex turned his head toward the tourists for help. Suddenly, he noticed one guy's T-shirt. It read, I LOVE NEW YORK!

"Hey!" Alex told the guy. "I love New York, too. It's me, Alex the—"

Fump! An apple was stuffed into Alex's mouth, shutting him up.

Alex couldn't believe his rotten luck. All he wanted to do was make his father proud. Now everything was about to go up in smoke!

Just when Alex felt like a roasted chestnut, someone crashed through the tourist camp gate. It wasn't Marty—it was Zuba!

"Lion!" the tourists cried.

Alex spit out the apple. "Dad!" he shouted.

With a flying leap Zuba knocked Alex from the fire. He slashed the ropes with his claws, setting Alex free.

The tourists circled Alex and Zuba.

"Stay behind me," Zuba told Alex. "I want you to run for it while I attack."

Alex's eyes moved back and forth between his dad and the humans. He knew he had to do *something*. So he began to dance!

"What are you doing, Son?" Zuba demanded.

"The only thing I know how to do!" Alex said.

The tourists watched as Alex broke into his famous number, just as he did back home in the zoo every single day.

"I know those moves," Staten Island Joe cried. "Alex?"

One by one the tourists dropped their spears.

"It's Alex the lion!"

"From the zoo!"

Alex knew he had the tourists in the palm of his paw. He kept on dancing as his audience smiled.

Then, out of nowhere—Zuba's feet started dancing, too!

"That's it, Dad," Alex urged. "Go with it!"

Zuba followed
Alex's lead. Soon
father and son
were fluttering
their paws,
twirling, kicking,
and launching into
a stunning spinning
leap!

"*Roar!*" Alex
shouted as he landed in
his famous pose.

"*Roar!*" Zuba
sang, too, posing in
perfect sync.

The tourists went
wild, cheering and
clapping for Alex
the King of New York.
Alex smiled as he

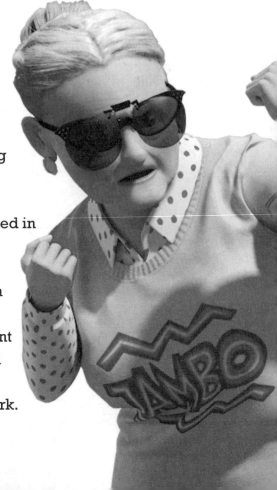

took a bow. But when he straightened up, he saw his old nemesis holding a salad bowl—it was Nana!

"What's all this?" she asked. Then she saw the lions. "Two bad kitties!" She started marching forward for another fistfight, but suddenly there was a shout from above.

Alex looked up. Waving from a monkey-powered plane in the sky was Marty. A chain of monkeys linked arm in arm stretched down from the hovering plane. The monkeys were holding on to a cut-off oil barrel, as if it were a basket.

"Alex, get in!" Marty yelled down. Alex and Zuba climbed into the barrel and were whisked into the air.

"Pass it up!" Alex told the lowest monkey on the barrel chain. "Get us to safety and we'll come back for the dam!"

The monkeys passed up Alex's message. But by the time it reached Marty it became: "Be hasty! Use us as a battering ram!"

"Skipper!" Marty called into the cockpit. "Alex wants to take out the dam!"

The penguin shook his head. It wasn't just the penguins flying this time . . . Melman and Gloria were fighting over the steering wheel.

"Give me that! You've never driven before," yelled Melman as he grabbed the wheel.

Exasperated, the hippo glared at him. "Snookims, you're being—"

Melman suddenly melted. "I'm your snookims?" he asked.

Gloria smiled back at him. "Yeah," she said sweetly.

Nana watched horrified as the plane turned around. Her dinner was getting away! She scrambled to the top of the dam. From there she watched as the plane flew closer and closer. When it was near, she shook her fist at them and shouted, "I'll show you hooligans!"

Alex groaned when he saw Nana. He shouted to Skipper to pull the plane up. But it was too late.

Alex and Zuba held on tight as the barrel rammed into the logs—and Nana!

Alex watched as water gushed past the fallen logs. He had saved the water hole. Now he had to save his friends and family from Makunga!

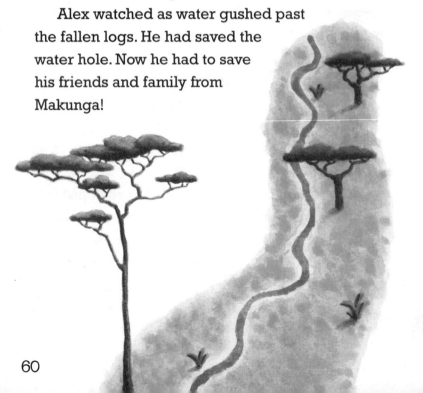

CHAPTER TEN

Meanwhile, back at the water hole, Makunga and Teetsi continued to guard the tiny puddle that was left. Makunga was dipping his paw in and sprinkling himself with drops of water.

"That hits the spot," he said to Teetsi.

The rest of the animals lay in the sun, parched tongues hanging out. Everyone was thirsty.

Suddenly there was a slow rumbling from the ground. A huge wave of water rushed in, with Alex and Zuba riding their barrel to shore.

"My son! He saved us all!" Zuba's voice shouted.

The animals cheered. "Thank you, Alakay! Yay!" Alex's mom stood at the edge of the now completely full water hole and yelled, "That's my baby!"

The two lions climbed out of the barrel and

turned around to see a very wet Makunga, who reminded Zuba that he had quit the pride and that Alex was kicked out. "Technically speaking," Makunga said coolly, "neither one of you can challenge me."

"Technically speaking," Alex said with a grin, "we're not going to challenge you . . ."

He knocked over the barrel and out popped Nana!

". . . she is!" Alex said.

Nana narrowed her eyes at Makunga. "Bad kitty!" she hissed.

Alex smiled as Makunga ran away and the old woman followed. Then he picked up the scepter and handed it back to his dad.

Everyone cheered as Zuba lifted the scepter in the air. Their beloved leader was back. And that called for another party around the water hole!